Dedicated to all those who have ever felt overlooked and unseen.
With love, JDS

S. D. G.
—RB

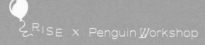

An Imprint of Penguin Random House LLC, New York

Text copyright © 2020 by Joshua David Stein. Illustrations copyright © 2020 by Ron Barrett.
All rights reserved. Published by Rise × Penguin Workshop, an imprint of
Penguin Random House LLC, New York. PENGUIN and PENGUIN WORKSHOP are
trademarks of Penguin Books Ltd. The W colophon is a registered trademark and the
RISE colophon is a trademark of Penguin Random House LLC. Manufactured in China.

Visit us online at www.penguinrandomhouse.com.

The text is hand-lettered and set in Adobe Hebrew.
The art was created using pen and ink, and colored in Photoshop.
Edited by Cecily Kaiser
Designed by Maria Elias

Library of Congress Control Number: 2019056131

ISBN 9780593222775   10 9 8 7 6 5 4 3 2 1

THE INVISIBLE ALPHABET

written by
JOSHUA
DAVID STEIN

illustrated by
RON
BARRETT

RISE

NEW YORK

A is for Air

B is for Bare

C is for Clear

D is for Delayed

E is for Erased

F is for Freed

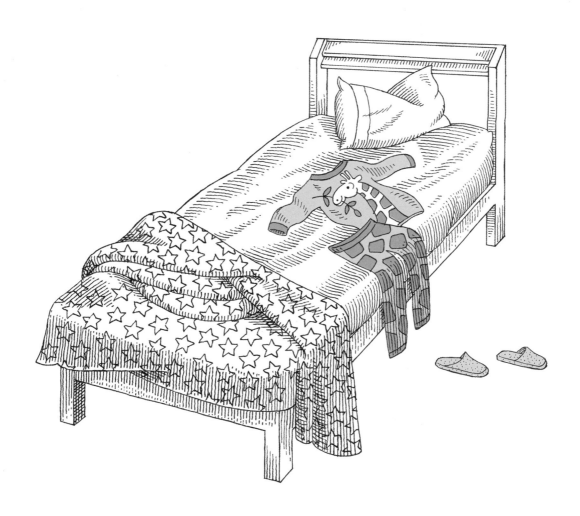

G is for Gone

H is for Hidden

I is for Invisible

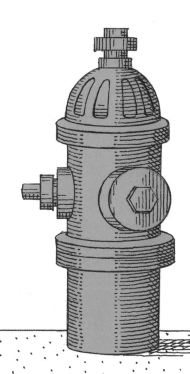

J is for Just missed it

K is for Knocked it out

L is for Lost

M is for Microscopic

N is for Nothing

O is for Out

P is for Popped

Q is for Quiet

R is for Ran away

S is for Secret

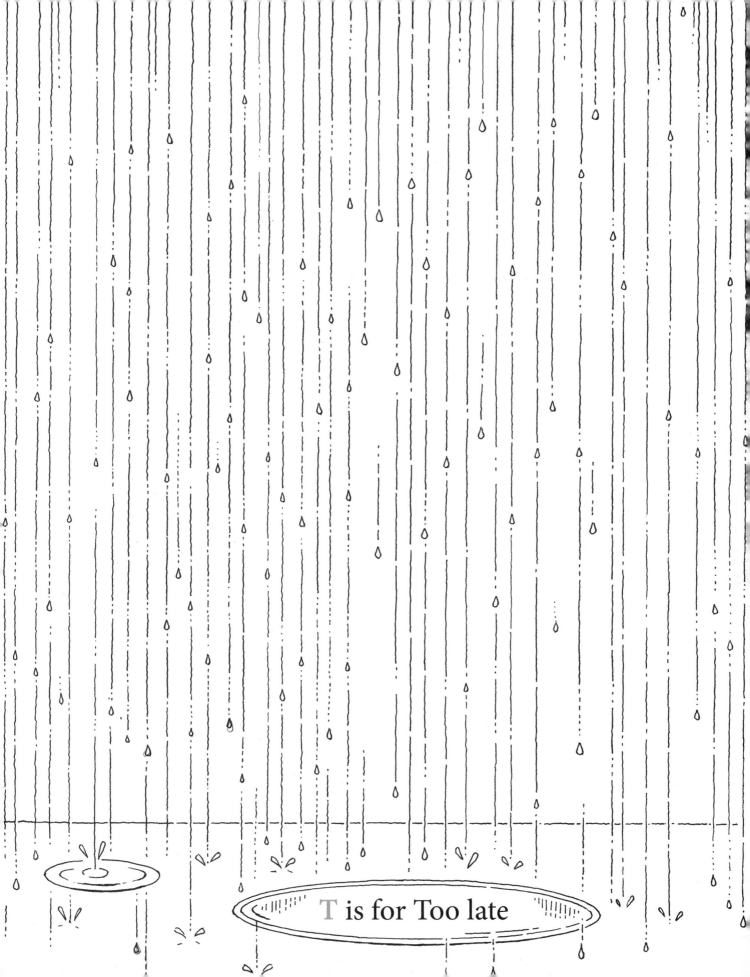

T is for Too late

U is for Unseen

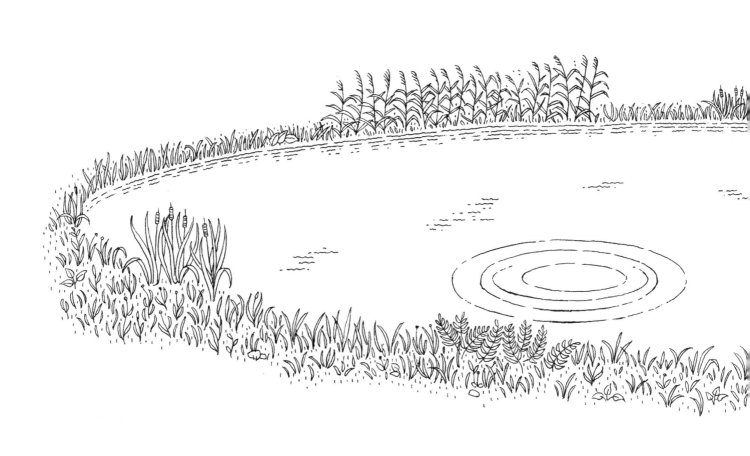

V is for Vanished

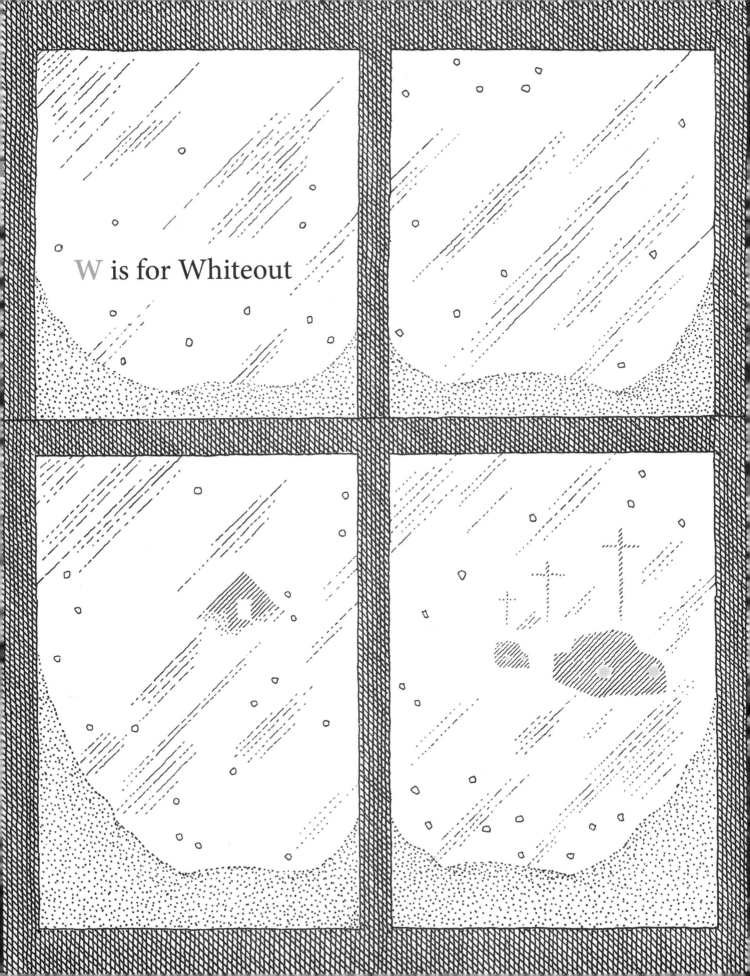

W is for Whiteout

X is in Extinguished

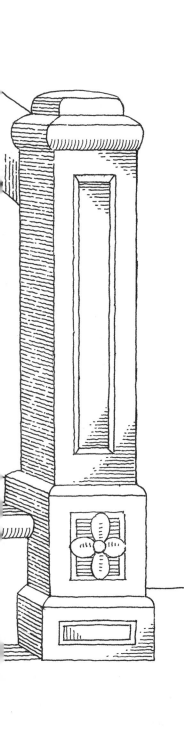

Y is for Yesterday

Z is for Zero